Page 2

Page 4

Page 6

Page 10

Page 11

Page 12

Page 14

Page 16

Page 17

Page 19

Page 20

Page 27

Page 28

Page 29

Page 30

Page 33

Page 34

Page 39

Page 42

Page 40

Page 43

Page 45

Page 49

Page 50

Page 54

Page 52

Page 55

Page 56

Page 58

FLYING HIGH

This fox soars through the sky in his airplane! Can you spot three differences in the second picture? Add a star sticker for each one you find.

PLAY BALL!

Draw a baseball field for these two players so the game can get under way.

PRETTY PATTERNS

Where there are flowers, there are sure to be butterflies! Find the sticker that goes next in each row.

1.

2.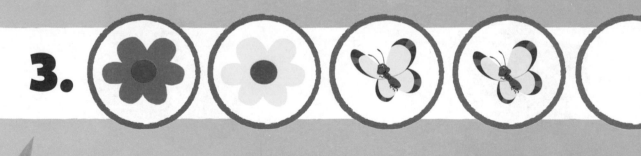

3.

4.

FRIENDLY FROGS

How many frogs do you see? Count and color each one.

I see _____ frogs.

Answer on page 63

AHOY, MATEYS!

Use your stickers to complete the picture of this fishy pirate!

Answer on page 63

BIKE RIDERS

Get the hedgehog bike rider to his friend
so they can ride together!

START

FINISH

Answer on page 63

MONSTER MATCH

Only two of these friendly monsters are exactly the same.
Draw a line between the two that match.

A WINNER IS SPOTTED!

Color this picture of the race winner. Why not make each spot a different color?

THREE BIRDS IN A ROW

Play this game with a friend. Decide who will be the red bird and who will be the blue bird. Take turns filling in spaces on the grid with your stickers. The winner is the first player to get three stickers in a row—up, down, across, or diagonally.

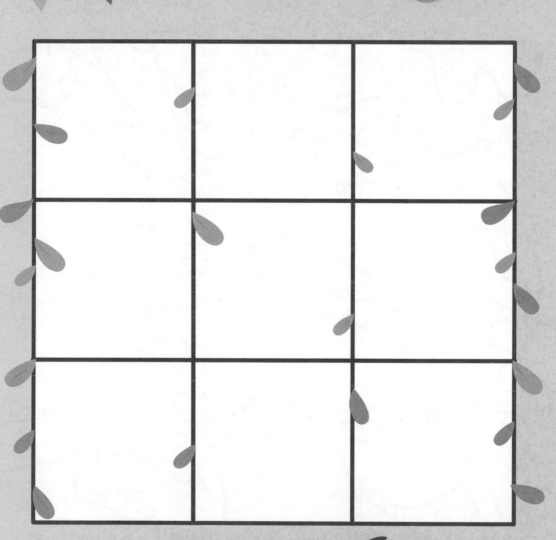

sweet treats

How many yummy cupcakes can you count in the picture?
Now use your stickers to make the total number of cupcakes 7.

Answer on page 63

A LeaFY LOOK

Two of these pictures of the happy, leaf-jumping squirrels are exactly the same. Stick a leaf sticker next to both of them.

WHO'S HeRE?

Unscramble the letters of the word for each animal and write the word correctly on the lines.

1. ACT

_ _ _

2. EPSHE

_ _ _ _ _

3. KANES

_ _ _ _ _

4. HIFS

_ _ _ _

Answers on page 63

READY TO RIDE

Draw a line to link each close-up with the correct vehicle.
Then add the matching stickers of the vehicles to the page.

A JUMBO SURPRISE

Connect the dots. Who do you see?

WEIGHT-LIFTING CHAMP

No one can lift more weight than this gorilla can! Give him a trophy sticker for his strength. Draw some bananas for him, too.

OUT-OF-THIS-WORLD MAIL

Pretend you are an astronaut and write a postcard to your best friend on Earth. Describe what you are seeing. Then, add a sticker stamp.

PLACE STAMP HERE

I SPY BUTTERFLIES!

Follow the flowers to get this zebra to the butterflies.

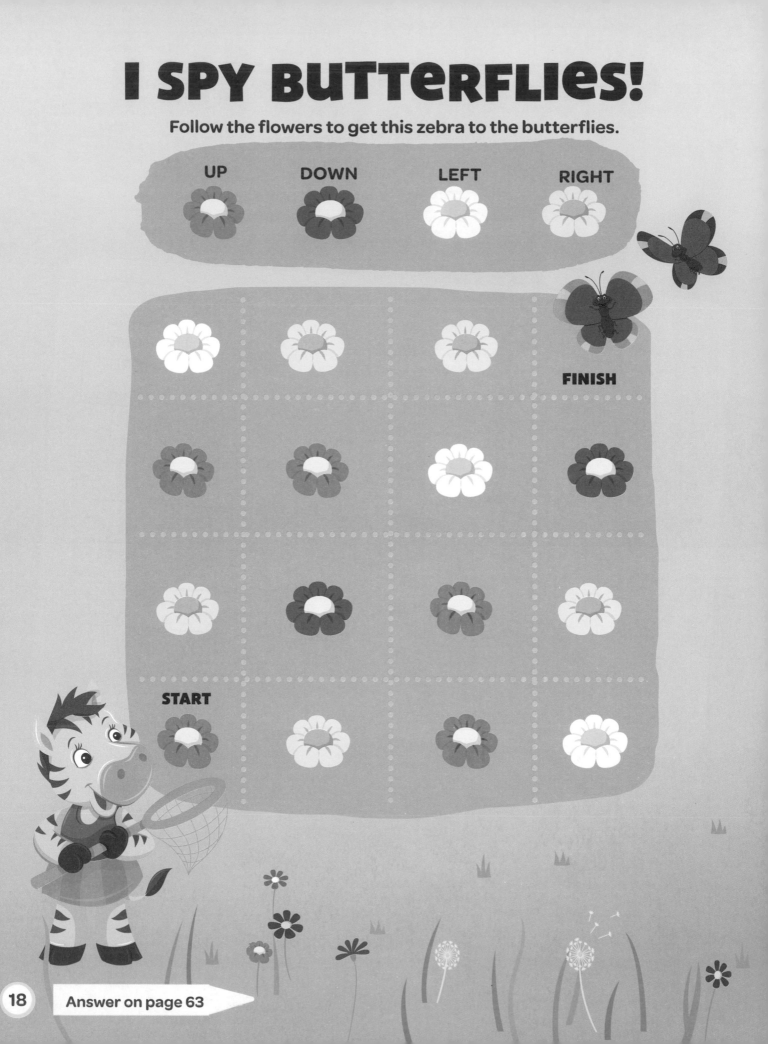

UNDERWATER ADVENTURE

Draw some interesting sea creatures for this scuba diver to discover, and add some stickers, too.

HI, BUTTERFLY!

Use the guide to complete the picture. Then, use your stickers to add more butterflies.

20

YUM!

Draw a big ice cream sundae for this lucky lizard to be licking.

WHICH WAY TO EARTH?

Which path will get this space traveler to planet Earth?

A.

B.

C.

Answer on page 63

IN HIS PAWS

What is the puppy holding in his paws? Write down the first letter and then every second letter in the circle to find out.

START HERE

S N O W B A L L

Answer on page 63   23

Dance, Dance, Dance!

Copy the colors on the opposite page to complete this picture of the dynamite dino dancer.

WRONG ROBOT

One of these robots is pretending to be just like the others, but he's a little different. Find him.

Answer on page 63

THREE JUNGLE CRITTERS

Each of these animals should appear once in each row and column. Use stickers to fill the empty squares.

Answers on page 63

JUMPING FOR JOY

Use your puzzle stickers to complete the picture
so you can see who is having some fun.

SLUMBER PARTY!

Add the sticker of this girl's best friend. She is so excited for their slumber party!

COLORFUL ROWS

Crayons come in so many colors. Find the sticker for the one that comes next in each row.

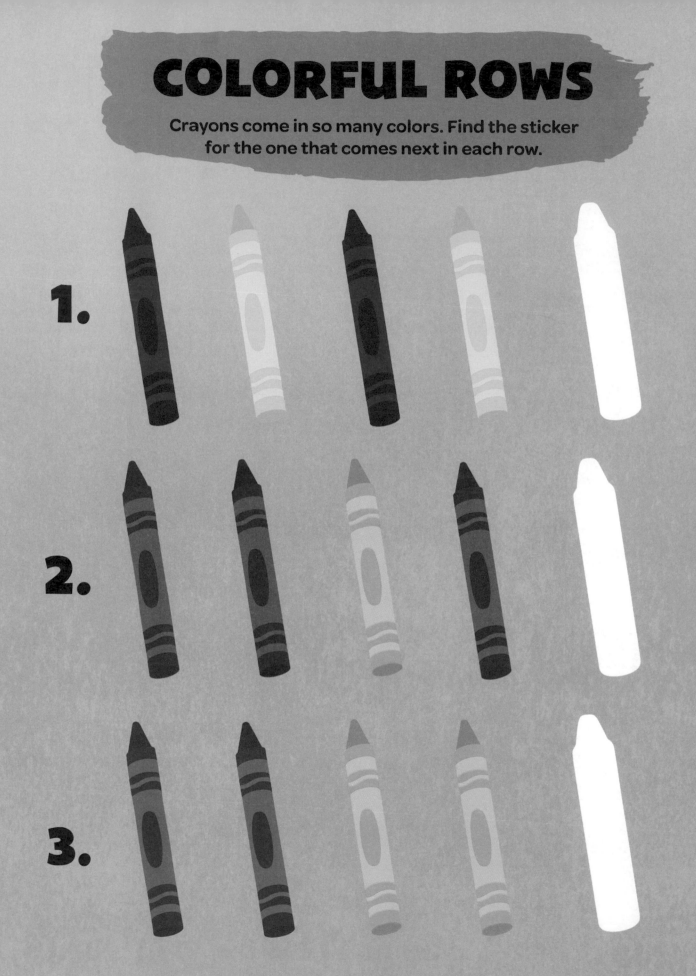

1.

2.

3.

ROAD TRIP

Nothing beats traveling with good friends! Can you find three things that are different in the second picture below?

PRETTY FLOWER!

Which two images of this sweet little guy and his pretty flower are exactly the same?

Answers on page 63

FaRM FRiENDS

Look at each of these silhouettes and find the matching sticker.
Place the stickers in the boxes.

we Love camping!

Color this cozy camp scene and add some stickers of buzzing bugs.

FRIENDS ON THE GO

Get this speed-demon chicken to his pogo-jumping pal.

TO THE RESCUE

Unscramble the names of these rescue vehicles and write them correctly on the lines next to each one.

ceilpo arc

_ _ _ _ _ _ _ _ _

echprteloi

_ _ _ _ _ _ _ _ _ _

ifre ktcur

_ _ _ _ _ _ _ _ _

HELLO!

Connect the dots to see who is waving to you.

WHERE'S THE PARTY?

Find and circle the two partygoers that are exactly the same.

MOOVING WORDS

Write a postcard to your favorite farm animal
and put a sticker stamp on it.

PLACE
STAMP
HERE

LOOKING FOR TREASURE

Give this pirate and her treasure map some bright colors.
Then, add a parrot sticker to the page.

Use the guide to complete the picture.

OUT FOR a DRIVE

Use your stickers to complete the picture of these birds flying down the highway.

Answer on page 64

A STAR COW

Give that cow a gold star sticker for jumping as high as the moon! Now count how many stars you see. Be sure to count the star sticker, too.

Answer on page 64

Rain Gear

Draw a line between each rainy-day item and the letter it starts with.

C

B

U

SOMETHING FISHY

One of these rows of fish is different from the others.
Find it and put a sea star sticker next to it.

1.

2.

3.

4.

Answer on page 64

HOT-AIR BALLOON RIDE

"Wow, what a view from up here!"

Copy the colors on the opposite page to complete this picture.

47

WANT TO PLAY?

Find and circle each of these musical instruments in the puzzle. Look up, down, left, right, and diagonally.

drum	tuba	guitar
banjo	flute	oboe

G	M	E	R	P	F
T	U	B	A	O	L
O	R	I	U	J	U
B	D	C	T	N	T
O	K	U	L	A	E
E	H	Y	I	B	R

APPLE PICKING

It's apple-picking time! How many apples do you see?
Add apple stickers so you have a total of 10.

Answer on page 64

ONe ODD BIRD

Which dancing flamingo is a little different?
Find him, and add a star sticker next to him.

Answer on page 64

NO PLACE LIKE HOME

Connect the dots so the hermit crab can enjoy his new home.

MAKING A SPLASH

Look at these animals having a good time in the water.
Use your stickers to place the matching shadow in each circle.

space walk

Follow the stars, moon, sun, and Earth to get the astronaut back to her space shuttle.

UP   DOWN   LEFT   RIGHT

START

FINISH

Answer on page 64   53

SHINING BRIGHTLY

How many lightning bugs do you see on the page?
Count them, then color the picture. Now add your
lightning bug stickers to get a total of 8.

 Answer on page 64

AT THE BEACH

Use your stickers to complete the picture
of this happy builder and his sandcastle.

Answer on page 64

TEST YOUR MEMORY

Take a good look at this picture. Then cover it up and see what you can remember about it. Place a check mark sticker in the circle that is correct about each statement.

	True	False
1. The dino is wearing a green shirt.	◯	◯
2. The dino is eating a donut.	◯	◯
3. The dino has three fins on his head.	◯	◯
4. The dino's mouth is closed.	◯	◯

 Answers on page 64

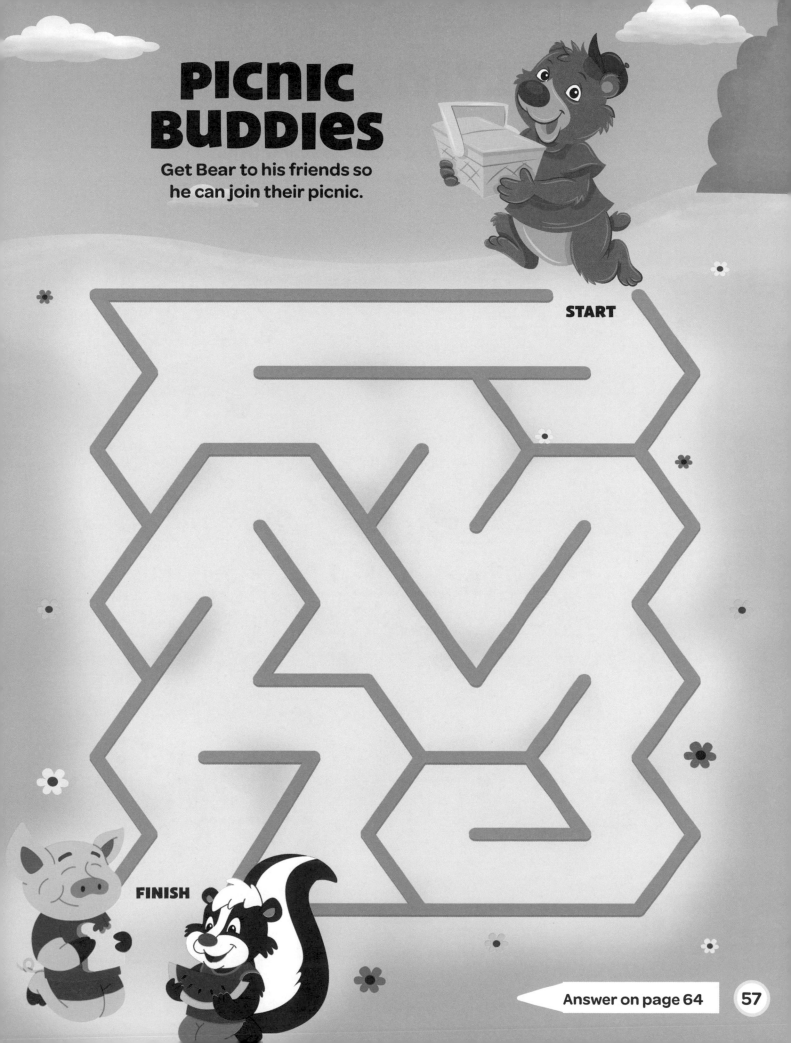

PICNIC BUDDIES

Get Bear to his friends so he can join their picnic.

START

FINISH

Answer on page 64

FLYING PIGS

One of these skydivers is a little different. Find him
and give him a bird sticker to soar with him.

Answer on page 64

YOUR WISH IS GRANTED!

Draw what you asked the genie for.

Draw a line to link each close-up with the correct athlete.

ON THE TRAIL OF CARROTS

Which path will get this carrot-loving rabbit to even more carrots?

A. B. C.

Answer on page 64

Which two of these traveling hippos are exactly the same?

Answers

Page 2

Page 4
1.
2.
3.
4.

Page 5 I see 6 frogs.

Page 6

Page 7

Page 8

Page 11 There are 3 cupcakes.

Page 12

Page 13
1. CAT
2. SHEEP
3. SNAKE
4. FISH

Page 14

Page 18

Page 22 Path B

Page 23 Snowball

Page 26

Page 27

Page 28

Page 30 1. 2. 3.

Page 31

Page 32

63

ANSWERS

Page 35

Page 36
1. police car
2. helicopter
3. fire truck

Page 38

Page 42

Page 43 There are 6 stars.

Page 44

Page 45 Row 3 is different.

Page 48

Page 49 There are 5 apples.

Page 50

Page 53

Page 54 There are 3 lightning bugs.

Page 55

Page 56
1. False
2. False
3. True
4. False

Page 57

Page 58

Page 60

Page 61 Path B

Page 62